Pedro the Brave

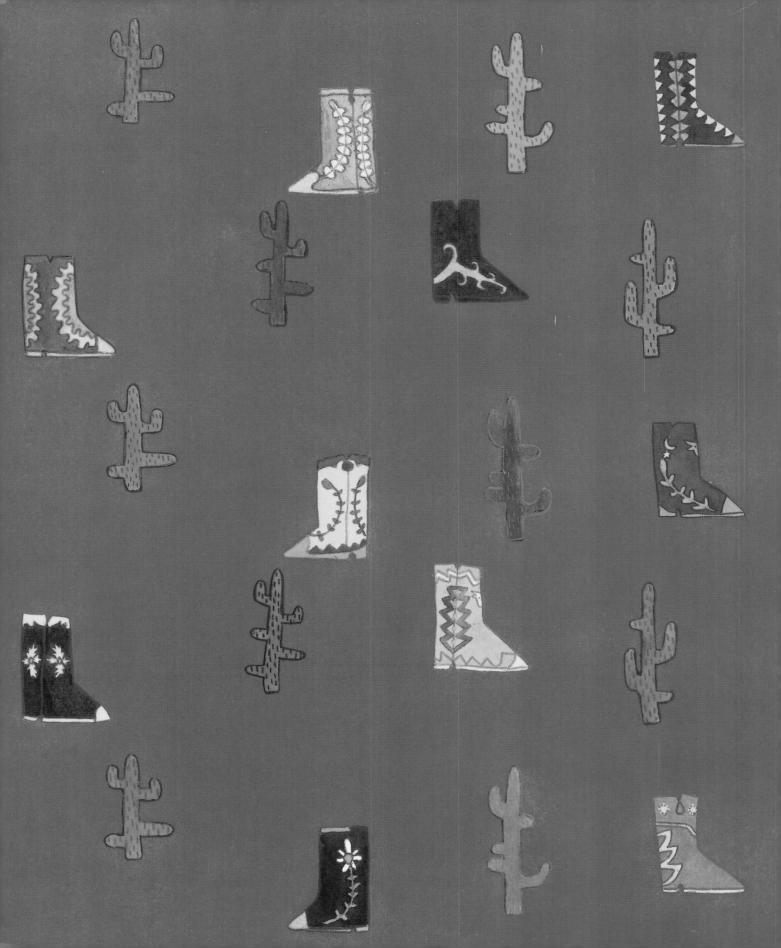

Pedro the Brave

Leo Broadley

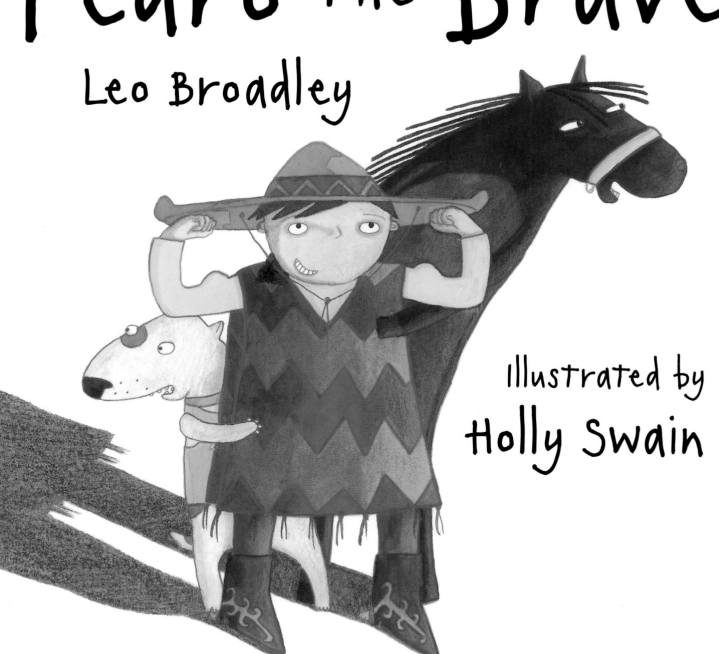

Illustrated by

Holly Swain

To Colin, Avril and Simon
who I love very much.
L.B.

To Daniel, Jasmine and Hannah.
May you all be as brave as Pedro.
H.S.

Scholastic Children's Books
Commonwealth House, 1-19 New Oxford Street,
London WC1A 1NU, UK
a division of Scholastic Ltd
London – New York – Toronto – Sydney – Auckland
Mexico City – New Delhi – Hong Kong

First published in hardback by Scholastic Ltd, 2002
This paperback edition published by Scholastic Ltd, 2002

Text copyright © Leo Broadley, 2002
Illustrations copyright © Holly Swain, 2002

0 439 98270 7

Printed by Oriental Press, Dubai, UAE
All rights reserved

1 3 5 7 9 10 8 6 4 2

The rights of Leo Broadley and Holly Swain to be identified respectively as the author
and illustrator of this work have been asserted by them in accordance with the
Copyright, Designs and Patents Act, 1988.

I'll tell you a story of Pedro the Brave
That will make all your whiskers go curly.
About using your wits to keep wolves from the door,
And why you should go to bed early.

It was one night in June, with a bright August moon,
Under millions of twinkling stars,
That Pedro and Dusty and Ronnie the horse
Were dancing and playing guitars.

ta da de daa
ta da de da

When there in the wood, a timber wolf stood,
With a tongue that was dripping and red.
He came to the fire and sat himself down.
"It's a fine night for singing," he said.

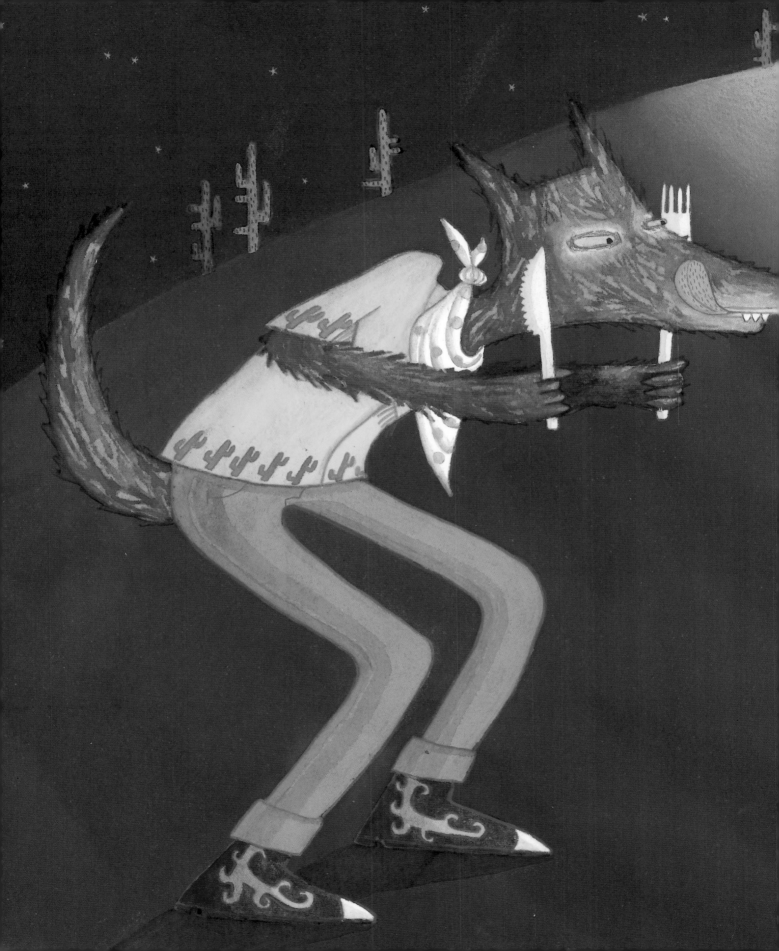

Now everyone knew that the wolf wanted meat,
And didn't know how to behave.
He wanted to gobble all three of them up –
It's a good thing that Pedro was brave.

"I have an idea!" Pedro said to his friends,
And he made up the stove nice and hot.
Then he turned to the wolf with a bow and he said,
"Would you kindly get
into the pot?"

"**What, me?**" cried the wolf.
"What on earth can you mean,
    to have such a foolish idea?
That I should be dinner for somebody else –
I do the eating round here."

"I'll do you a deal,"
said Pedro the Brave.
"If I'm going to be the first course,
I'll jump in this pan with no fuss at all,
If you'll just let me cook my own sauce."

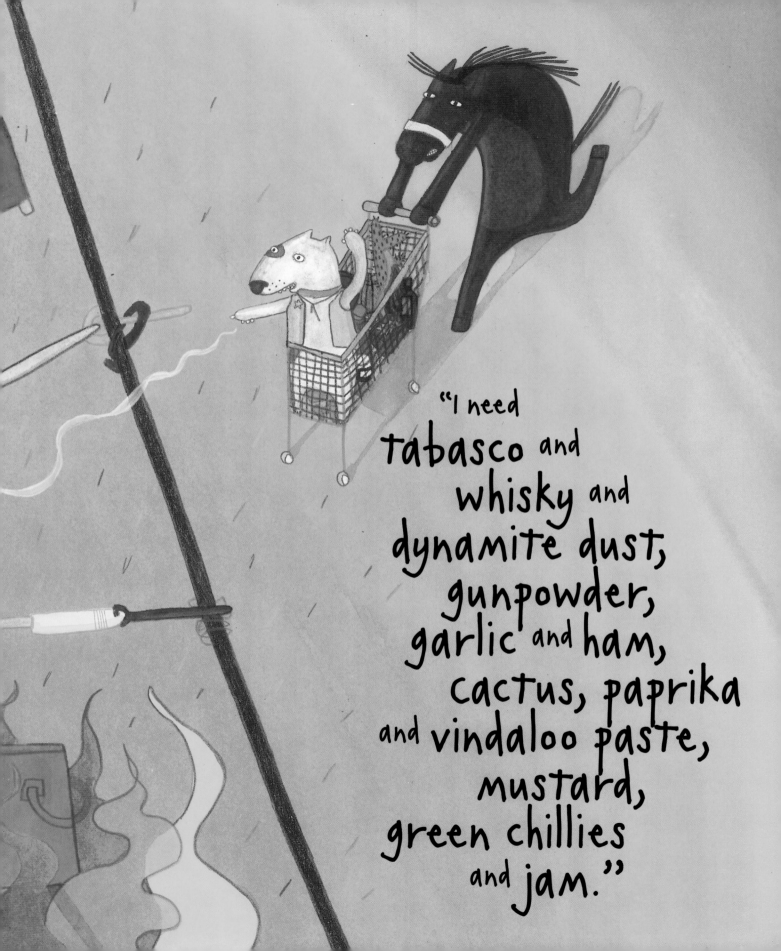

"I need
tabasco and
whisky and
dynamite dust,
gunpowder,
garlic and ham,
cactus, paprika
and vindaloo paste,
mustard,
green chillies
and jam."

Pedro turned to the wolf and he said, with a smile,
"Before I add me to your diet,
Just put a drop of this sauce on your tongue –
I'm eager for someone to try it."

Now when I say it was hot, it really was HOT,
It was hotter than flames on your toes.
It blew the wolf's socks off, his shirt and his pants,
It shot flames from the end of his nose.

"I feel ill," moaned the wolf, "and
my mouth is on fire,
There are bombs going bang in my head.
I feel like I've eaten some firework pie -
I'll go and eat ice-cream instead!"

Pedro the Brave put some wood on the fire.
"Now before everyone goes to bed,
Pick up your guitars under twinkling stars –
It's a fine night for singing,"
he said.